The
Art Nouveau
Fairy Tale

Coloring Book

~

by Laura Givens

Published by

www.dreamsalvage.com

ISBN: 0692745823

ISBN-13: 978-0692745823 (Dream Salvage)

Introduction

Color me a story...

The most wonderful part of being read to as a child was reveling in the colorful illustrations that always accompanied the best stories. They would forever transform an improbable tale of fairies and handsome princes into an absolute truth. Because that is what fairy tales are — truth. All the witches and wolves are just the sugar that helps the medicine of morals go down, and, (to quote Ms. Poppins) in a most delightful way.

Stories like these teach us how to be human beings. They are the first stories we usually learn and they are primal. They can be told a thousand different ways and still retain their integrity.

The illustrations in this book are meant to allow you to tell these tales as you envision them. Perhaps you prefer bright Disney hues and warm tones—or maybe you like your yarns to be in a more Grimm palette, depressing even (Yes, I'm looking at you Hans Christian!). It's all good.

Why Art Nouveau? First conceived a century ago, it is a style that celebrates a playful, passionate immersion into its intricacies. It provides the repetition, detail and flow that best personify what a good adult coloring book should be.

Coloring books for adults have become a big deal. They are psychologically calming and can facilitate a meditative state. They provide a focus to tap into our creative potential and allow us to tune out the crazy world that constantly assaults us. Coloring books are non-judgmental, there is no right or wrong way to color them. It's true, coloring books can be very therapeutic... YUP!

But, let us not forget, coloring is fun. Ask any kid, ask every kid. Coloring is universally loved by children because it's fun. Too many adults have forgotten the sheer joy of playing just for the fun of it, so good for you, you coloring rebel.

I hereby declare that it is okay to color, to play and to have fun again, no matter what your age. So put on your fuzzy slippers, pour a glass of wine and color yourself a story.

It's cheaper than psychoanalysis.

- Laura Givens, June 2016

The Frog Prince

Jack and the Beanstalk

Ali Baba and the 40 Thieves

Sleeping Beauty

King Midas

Perseus and Medusa

Puss in Boots

Aladdin

Cinderella

Androcles and the Lion

The Pied Piper

Thumbelina

John Henry

Beauty and The Beast

Hansel and Gretel

The Brave Tin Soldier

Goldilocks and the 3 Bears

Pandora's Box

The Nightingale

Pinocchio

The Flight of Icarus

The Little Mermaid

The Goose Girl

Theseus and the Minotaur

Red Riding hood

Prometheus Brings Fire

Sheherazade

The Emperor's New Clothes

The Boy Who Cried Wolf

Snow White and the Seven Dwarves

The Shoemaker and the Elves

Orpheus and Eurydice

The Princess and the Pea

Pegasus and Bellerophon

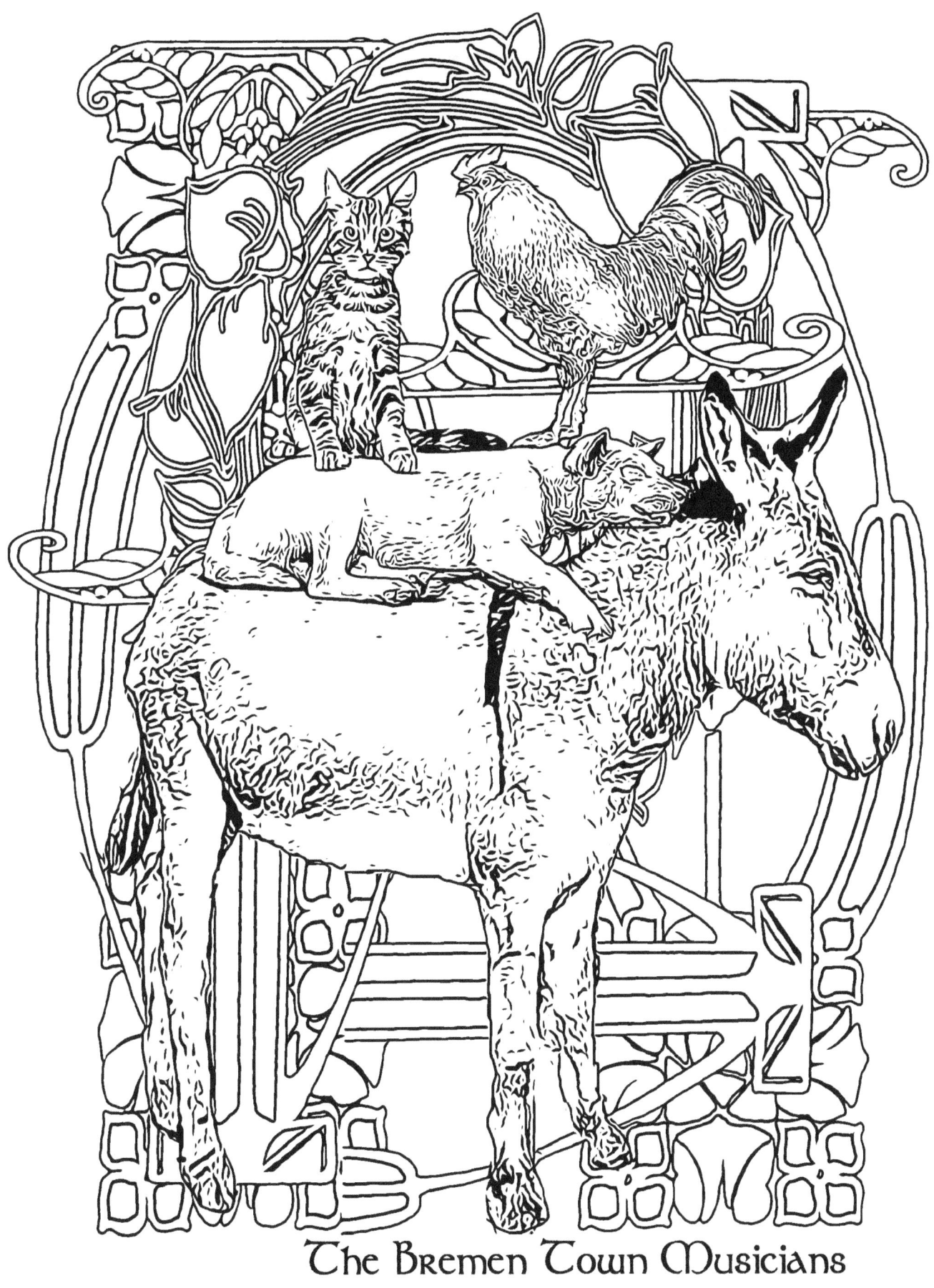

The Bremen Town Musicians

Rapunzel

The Snow Queen

Sinbad the Sailor

Rumplestiltskin

The Ugly Duckling

About the Artist

~

Laura Givens lives in Denver, Colorado where she never seems to find the time to actually get up into the Rocky Mountains — sigh. An artist, designer and illustrator, she has created book and magazine covers, as well as the occasional interior illustration, for a large number of publishers all over the world. She has created covers for genres as diverse as Science fiction, Fantasy, Horror, Romance, Poetry, Westerns and Weird Westerns. You may view these and her other work at her portfolio site, lauragivens-artist.com.

Laura is also a short story author whose stories have seen publication in anthologies, magazines and ebook collections. One of her stories, "The Fortress of Solicitude," has also been adapted to audio. All of her published stories have been collected into a book entitled *Crisis Averted*.

Please contact Laura through her Facebook page, "Laura Givens - Artist."